NORWICH JP
Page, Gail,
Bobo and the new neighbor
/

APR 1 0 2009

DATE DUE			
Purple crayon markings on 1st page 8/15/14			

. 2/11/09
8/15/14
④
2 owners

.KD

For Logan Page Fordham

Bobo
and the
NEW NEIGHBOR

by Gail Page

FOR
SALE

SOLD

BLOOMSBURY
CHILDREN'S
BOOKS

Bobo was a good dog.

He loved getting his picture taken.

He loved
taking long walks.

He loved saying hello to the mailman.

And he especially loved to share.

One day, someone new moved in next door.

That was another thing Bobo loved—
meeting new people.

So when Mrs. Birdhead decided to invite Mrs. Wrinklerump over for tea,

Bobo wanted to help.

Things didn't go so well.

"Out!" said Mrs. Birdhead.
"Go bring in the laundry."

Bobo **wanted** to help, but how was he going to carry all the laundry?

Aha!

He'd wear it, of course.

Opening the door
could have been tricky.
Luckily, Mrs. Birdhead
was there.

"How nice to meet you, Mrs. Wrinklerump,"
said Mrs. Birdhead. "Please come in."

Bobo was going to tell Mrs. Birdhead that he wasn't the new neighbor, but then he smelled

the muffins.

"I'll go get the tea," said Mrs. Birdhead.

"**Please** help yourself to a muffin."

So Bobo did.

Cat was suspicious.

The new neighbor had an enormous appetite.

Hmm. The new neighbor had **floppy** ears and **furry** paws and a **big black nose.**

The new neighbor was . . .

...an IMPOSTER!

Suddenly, the doorbell rang.

DING
DONG!

It was the **REAL** Mrs. Wrinklerump!

Bobo knew he had to act fast.

DING
DONG,

DING
DONG,

"Hello," said the person at the door.
"I'm Mrs. Wrinklerump."

Bobo and Cat were happy to show
the new neighbor to the table.

Just then, Mrs. Birdhead returned
with the tea. Strangely, there
was only one muffin left.

Bobo loved muffins,
but he loved new neighbors too.

So he did the only thing he could.
He shared.

Good dog, Bobo!

The end. Good-bye. Come again.

Art created with acrylics · Typeset in McKracken · Book design by Lilyzebra

Published by Bloomsbury U.S.A. Children's Books
175 Fifth Avenue, New York, New York 10010

Library of Congress Cataloging-in-Publication Data
Page, Gail.
Bobo and the new neighbor / Gail Page—1st U.S. ed.
p.   cm.
Summary: When Bobo the dog tries to help Mrs. Birdhead welcome a new neighbor,
he is soon up to his snout in hot water.
ISBN-13: 978-1-59990-009-4 · ISBN-10: 1-59990-009-2 (hardcover)
ISBN-13: 978-1-59990-315-6 · ISBN-10: 1-59990-315-6 (reinforced)
[1. Dogs—Fiction. 2. Neighbors—Fiction. 3. Cats—Fiction. 4. Humorous stories.] I. Title.
PZ7.P1377Bo 2008   [E]—dc22   2007052164

First U.S. Edition 2008
Printed in China
2 4 6 8 10 9 7 5 3 1 (hardcover)
2 4 6 8 10 9 7 5 3 1 (reinforced)

© **Mixed Sources**
Product group from well-managed
forests, controlled sources and
recycled wood or fibre
www.fsc.org Cert no. SCS-COC-00927
FSC © 1996 Forest Stewardship Council